The Mitcham Murder Mystery

By G. H. Teed

Author of
"MYSTERY ON THE BROADS," "THE USURPER,"
ETC.

FIRST PUBLISHED BY
MELLIFONT PRESS, 1935.

Stillwoods Edition, 2019.

Stillwoods.Blogspot.Ca

Catalogue Information:
Title: The Mitcham Murder Mystery
Author: G. H. Teed (1886-1938)
Author of "MYSTERY ON THE BROADS," "THE USURPER," ETC.
First published by: Mellifont Press, 1935
This Edition by: Stillwoods, 2019.
ISBN Canada: 978-1-988304-86-1
Blog: Stillwoods.Blogspot.Ca
Author Blog: http://ghteed.blogspot.com/
Storefront: http://www.lulu.com/spotlight/lulubook22

Keywords: Lawrence Malone, British fictional detective,

Lawrence Malone, private detective is hired by the three Crabbe brothers who believe they will be charged with the murder of their uncle.

The case is almost open-and-shut against the youngest, a reckless lad.

One complication is that there appeared to be no exit available to the killer. In any case, there are forces which don't want Malone to be on this mystery. His life is in peril.

Worldcat.Org lists only one copy of this murder mystery by Teed, worldwide. It is at The British Library, St. Pancras. When I saw it available through a used bookdealer, I had to get the copy. Someday that copy will probably reside back in Teed's home province—at the Archives of New Brunswick which actually holds books at the University of New Brunswick in Fredericton.

Overleaf are some titles from Mellifont Press in 1935.

Similarly see the last page.

OTHER TITLES IN THIS SERIES

ART COLOURED COVERS. 64 pp. Best Authors

Bottom of Suez
Crooks' Vendetta
Voodoo Island
Five in Fear
The Grey Ghost
The Case of the Duplicate Key
The Temple of Many Visions
Gangland's Decree
The Clue of the Four Wigs
The Mystery of the Film City
The Black Abbot
Murder Ship
Spies Ltd.
A Mystery of the Big Woods
The Mystery of the Kidnapped Killer
The Secret of the Swamp
The Case of the Pink Macaw
The Terror of Gold-digger Creek
The Case of the Mummified Hand
Pearls of Doom
The Victim of the Gang
The Case of the Courtlandt Jewels
Nelson Lee and the Lhassa Red Menace
The Riddle of the Russian Gold
Voodoo Vengeance
Hounded Down
Bribery and Corruption
The Sacred Sphere
The Tiger of Canton
The Crook of Marsden Manor
The Affair of the Six Ikons
The Secret of the Coconut Groves
The Case of the Disguised Apache
Under the Eagles Wing
The Rogues' Republic

CHAPTER ONE

When news of murder at Mitcham came through to Scotland Yard, Inspector Latham was in conference with Superintendent Wright. The report was accompanied by a request from the Chief Constable of Surrey that Scotland Yard would send an officer at once to take over the inquiry.

"This is your meat, Latham," Wright said. "This other matter can wait. You'd better get along at once and see what it is. Make your own arrangements."

At Mitcham, Latham was given brief particulars of the murder. The local inspector seemed relieved that the Yard had sent Latham, one of their most experienced men.

"We made the discovery a little after ten last evening," he told him. "The divisional surgeon, however, puts the time of death about two hours earlier. Shall I give you a brief outline here? Or would you prefer to go straight on to the spot?"

"I'll have an outline here."

"The victim was a retired solicitor named Jacob Crabbe. We had no personal knowledge about him. He seems to have lived very quietly in a villa in Sutton Road. As far as we can gather at present, he was unmarried and lived alone except for a housekeeper and a general maid, who were both out last evening when the crime occurred."

"Alibis?"

"We haven't checked up yet, but they seem sound enough."

"We can attend to that later. Go on, please."

"The maid came in at half-past nine and went straight to bed. She didn't see anything of her master, but took it for granted that he was in his study where, it seems, he spent most of his time reading and writing. His housekeeper returned a few minutes after ten. In accordance with what she says was her usual custom, she knocked at the door of the study to ask if her employer wanted anything before she went to bed. She got no answer. When she had knocked several times and still got no response, she tried the door. It was locked on the inside. Thinking that he might be asleep she hammered harder on the door, but without any result. She says she became uneasy then and decided to call a neighbour, an elderly man who lives two doors away and with whom, as far as we can gather, the dead man was on some sort of friendly terms."

"He wasn't much of a mixer, then?"

"On the contrary, he appears to have been well named. This one person, another retired fellow, was the only one he had any friendly association with, and 1 understand that he even quarrelled with him more often than not."

"Umph! Seems to have been an unpleasant character. If he had no friends, did he have any enemies?"

"Possibly," conceded the local inspector cautiously. "I'll come to that later. I think we can find a motive along that line. But to get back to the actual crime. When the housekeeper brought the neighbour along and still no response came to their hammering, it was decided to inform the police. A telephone message was received here at a quarter past ten. I happened to be here. I decided to go on myself and investigate. When I could get no satisfaction by knocking, I forced the door. And then it was plain enough why the door hadn't been opened. The man was sitting at the desk, lying forward so that his face rested on the blotting pad. The arms of the chair had kept him from slipping to the floor.

"And it was murder, all right. Someone had driven a knife into his back, so that it opened up the heart. It had been stabbed with such force that only the handle protruded, those are the bare facts."

"You say the doctor puts the time of death at two hours or so before the body was found."

"Yes."

"And the door was locked on the inside!"

"Yes."

"What about windows?"

"There are two. They were both secured on the inside. That's why we asked the Yard to send someone. This job is the toughest one I've ever seen."

"Is there another door?"

"No. The one opening on to the hall and the two windows are the only means of ingress and egress."

"And you say the victim was stabbed in the back, with the door and windows in that condition?"

"Yes,"

Latham rose.

"I think I'd like to see the room before we go any further."

Inspector Garthwaite rose with him.

"I'll take you along at once."

"Mon Repos," the villa where the crime had occurred, was a small, neat house in its own garden at the very end of Sutton Road. A rather thick belt of trees and a high hedge gave it more seclusion than any of the other houses in the road.

One could place the residents as belonging to the modestly well-to-do middle class though it was not unusual, Latham knew, to find that there was considerable means behind such a modest front. He was to discover, before many hours passed, that the murdered man, Jacob Crabbe, was one of this sort, for his financial resources were to be revealed as something in the neighbourhood of one hundred thousand pounds. But, at the moment, the house into which they entered presented no more luxury than might have been found in that of a retired tradesman of careful habits.

A few morbidly curious persons were gathered at the gate inside which a constable was on guard. Another constable admitted them to the house, which, Inspector Latham found, consisted of four rooms and a kitchen on the ground floor. These comprised a small drawing-room or parlour that was cold and cheerless with the air being little used, a dining-room, furnished in heavy, depressing style, a small sitting-room which, Latham found, was used by the housekeeper, and the study in which the murdered man had been found.

This room showed many signs of having been in constant use by the owner. It was crowded with furniture. The walls were lined with books, most of them heavy volumes belonging to the law library that had been brought along from Crabbe's offices when he retired. The desk was a litter of papers. Books and papers lay strewn about the floor. Pipes and tobacco tins made an untidy mess in almost every available spot. And, in the midst of this untidiness, on a battered leather couch against the wall, lay the body of the murdered man.

Latham drew down the sheet that covered it and made a brief examination. The doctor's report would tell him all he needed to know about that phase of the matter. The knife with which the murder had been done lay on a sheet of clean paper on the desk. Apart from the moving of the body, everything had been left just as it had been found by Garthwaite.

Latham's most immediate concern was the door and windows.

A brief survey of the room showed him that, as Garthwaite had said, there was no means of ingress or egress other than that way.

The lock of the door had, of course, been smashed to gain an entry, but the window-catches were still secured and a preliminary scrutiny failed to give Latham any encouragement.

Garthwaite made no suggestions. He was content to leave it to the man from Scotland Yard to carry on in his own way. There was no petty jealousy about Garthwaite. He was only too pleased to have the privilege of working with the famous Latham.

Whatever he might have gathered at the end of his tour, Latham gave no hint, he simply told Garthwaite that he wanted to telephone to the Yard for a certain expert. The local inspector had seen him devoting some attention to a locked safe in one corner and had little trouble in deducing that Latham intended having it opened as soon as possible.

When the message had been sent, and, as Garthwaite had thought, a lock expert instructed to come along from the Yard, Latham led the way into the dining room.

"Now for the persons in the house and the neighbour who was summoned," he said crisply. "I think we'll take the statements of the housekeeper and the maid first."

Garthwaite sent a constable to fetch them from the kitchen. The housekeeper appeared first. Latham gave her a quick but comprehensive scrutiny.

He saw a tall, good-looking woman with an excellent figure and, he thought, somewhat better dressed than one would expect to find in a person of her station at that hour of the morning. It was not yet mid-day. She was quite composed and met his gaze with a pair of blue eyes that did not waver.

It was plain that the presence of the police held no terrors for her.

Latham, who was, of necessity, a quick and correct reader of persons, sized her up instantly as a woman of plenty of decision of character and shrewd understanding. He told himself that, in her, he ought to find a witness of intelligence.

But, to his quick amazement, it was not he who was to open the interview in his usual tactful manner. No sooner had Garthwaite informed the woman that Latham was direct from Scotland Yard and desired to hear her statement than she turned her shoulder, ignoring Garthwaite utterly.

"So you are an officer of Scotland Yard?" she demanded of Latham.

Latham murmured an assent.

"Well, I'm glad you've come," she went on. "I've made a partial statement to this officer because they pestered me. But I knew someone higher would come along and I've saved my full statement until now."

"Your full statement, madam?"

"Exactly. I can tell you who murdered Mr. Crabbe."

CHAPTER TWO

Astonishment is hardly the word to describe Latham's feelings on hearing this amazing statement made in tones of cool certainty. He was flabbergasted. Never, in the whole course of his long career in the investigation of crime had he come up against anything quite like this. And he realised that, in making the statement, the woman was not being idly sensational. She had something definite to say and he had a hunch that it might be worth listening to.

But he betrayed none of this surprise. Latham had encountered too many bombshells to bat an eye at a new one.

"Won't you sit down, Mrs. —. I'm afraid I didn't catch your name."

She sank into a chair.

"My name is Clara Deason—Mrs. Clara Deason."

"You are a widow?"

"I am."

"Well, Mrs. Deason, you have just made a rather remarkable statement. Will you please explain what it means?"

"It means just what it says. Maybe I can't tell you which one of the three did it, but it was one of them."

"One of which three, madam? You must agree that this is somewhat confusing to me."

"One of the nephews, of course."

Latham glanced at Garthwaite. It was plain that the local inspector was as much in the dark as himself. He knew it would not help to urge the woman to make haste in telling her story. Such a prodding would be more likely to cause her to close up entirely. So he waited. And, after a few minutes silence, the story came.

"It was one of the three nephews," Mrs. Deason went on and now the two police officials could detect a strong acid tone in her voice. "I knew ever since the last quarrel that something would happen. You get those three and you'll find that one or all of them did this thing."

"Let me understand this, please," coaxed Latham. "You say that Mr. Crabbe had three nephews with whom he had quarrelled!"

"Isn't that what I've just been telling you!"

"How long ago did this quarrel take place?"

"About two months ago. It was the worst and last."

"There were other quarrels, then!"

The woman looked at Latham sourly.

"There were quarrels every time they came to the house."

Latham decided that they were getting nowhere. It was time, he thought, that a little Scotland Yard authority was displayed. He rose, dominating the woman from this position.

"I want you to listen to what I have to say," he told her curtly. "I am an officer from Scotland Yard called in on an official inquiry into what seems to be murder. You, as the housekeeper to the deceased, are a material witness. You have stated that you could name the person who committed the murder. You make general accusations against three persons whom you state were nephews of the deceased. Now I want from you a full statement, in terms as brief as possible, of just what you are able to tell us. We shall arrive at results more quickly by means of question and answer. If you propose delaying me then I must adopt other means to reach my objective. Do you understand?"

Mrs. Deason nodded sulkily.

"Go ahead with your questions."

"Very well. To begin with, how long have you occupied your present position?"

"Two years or more."

"During that time the internal conditions of the house were the same?"

"There's been a change of maids several times."

"How long has the present one been here?"

"About three months."

"You gave Inspector Garthwaite to understand in what you told him last night that the deceased had few intimate friends?"

"No one ever came but Mr. Gieves, who lives two doors along."

"I understand he is elderly."

"He is between seventy and eighty."

"What were the exact relations between him and your master!"

The woman's chin came up suddenly.

"Master, indeed! I'll have you to understand that I was to be married to Mr. Crabbe. As things are, I am the mistress of this house. You'll find that he left everything to me."

"Ah!"

Latham looked at her thoughtfully. What she had just said threw an entirely different light on the situation. If it were true then he began to understand her attitude.

"Was the wedding to be soon?"

"Some time next month. That's why they murdered him."

"You are referring again to the nephews?"

"Of course."

"Then we shall have particulars about them now. I want you to tell me as much as possible. What is their name?"

"Crabbe, same as their uncle's."

"Are they in business?"

"One is a solicitor. He took over his uncle's business when he retired. One is an architect. The other isn't anything—just a waster who lives by his wits. He's the one, in my opinion, who committed the murder."

Latham glanced at Garthwaite, who was busily taking notes. Latham knew he would attend to the detail of locating the three men whom the woman accused so definitely.

Then there came a tale of visits paid to the uncle by the nephews, of their attempts to borrow money from the uncle, of heated scenes between him and the youngest when he refused to advance further sums and, finally, of a terrific upheaval two months before when he had finally forbidden the youngest nephew the house and the latter had gone away muttering threats. Even when he had allowed for her very obvious hatred of the nephews, Latham realised that, with so much smoke there must be a considerable amount of fire. And, of course, it should not be difficult to get confirmation of her story.

"What was the cause of the last quarrel?" he asked after a pause. "Was it money again?"

"That, and being told that none of them would inherit a penny of his money."

"It had been arranged, then, that you were to marry?"

"Yes, and they knew that would finish them here."

"Had it not been for the marriage arranged with you, the nephews, I take it, would have inherited as next-of-kin?"

"They thought so, but Mr. Crabbe would have left his money somewhere else, I believe."

Latham let that go. From what he had been able to observe so far it did not seem that the dead man would have had more than a decent amount to leave, certainly not a fortune that would be large enough to inspire murder on the part of disappointed nephews no matter how violent of character they might be. And he was remembering that two of them, at least, were members of highly respectable professions. He did not know then of the surprising thing that they were to find in the safe.

He decided to suspend the questioning of the housekeeper then, merely asking her, as a matter of form (he explained) to account for her movements on the evening of the murder.

"I was with my sister, who is an invalid," she told him. "She lives in another part of Mitcham. I went straight there when I left the house a little after six, and I was there until I returned about ten."

"And the maid?"

"She was at the pictures with a friend."

"I'll just take her statement, I think."

But he abandoned the intention then, for at that moment the lock expert arrived from the Yard. He dismissed the housekeeper with a warning that he would want to speak to her later, then he and Garthwaite went into the study to watch the expert at work.

The safe was small and of ancient pattern. To the man who knelt before it, the job was as simple as going through a loaf of cheese with a sharp knife. Within three minutes he had the door swinging open with not a scratch to show.

Then Latham began to make an inventory of the contents and a quarter of an hour later, when he had finished, he had made two amazing discoveries.

One was to find a total in bonds, deeds, shares and government certificates of more than one hundred thousand pounds. It was astounding to know that this man who had lived in retirement in such a modest way had been possessed of wealth to that amount and in such gilt edge form.

There was, too, a bank book showing a liquid balance of some ten thousand pounds. It certainly caused him to regard motive from a very different angle and, remembering what the housekeeper had said, it was not difficult to see that such a prize was sufficient to arouse the cupidity of many a man.

The other discovery was the draft of a will. The wording of this confirmed in every respect what Mrs. Deason had said for in it, Jacob Crabbe left all his real and personal property of every sort to his housekeeper, Clara Deason.

But the will; was not signed.

CHAPTER THREE

Mr. Lawrence Malone stood at the window of his sitting-room in Adam Street gazing at the long, airlined red sports car that stood at the kerb.

It was just off the stand from the Motor Show at Olympia and, other than its immaculate newness of condition and model, was the same make and colour which he had favoured for some years. It was, indeed, a commonplace saying among members of London's criminal underworld that both Laurence Malone and his car were "crimson perils."

In both hands he held a lovely lacquered mascot in the form of a diving egret that had arrived by that morning's post from a wealthy Chinese merchant to whom he had recently been of some service in a most delicate matter. And he was interested to judge how it would look at the front of a super-long bonnet that now supported a silver cobra with hood expanded and head held ready for striking.

He was thus in an excellent position to watch the approach of another car that drew into the kerb just behind his own and to study at some leisure the three men who got out and, after a brief consultation, started for his own steps.

He saw, firstly, that they all appeared to be prosperous individuals and, two of them, he had little difficulty as placing as professional men. They were dressed in dark, formal attire and had that air stamped upon them which is the trade-mark of every calling and profession.

The third, however, was less easy to place. He had more the air of a devil-may-care fellow whose companions would have seemed more fitting had they been of the type who frequent the racecourses or betting clubs rather than the two obviously respectable professional men who walked one on either side of him.

Yet there was a pronounced likeness of feature about all three and, as he gave them swift appraisal, Lawrence Malone had little difficulty in placing it as fraternal or some other close kinship.

Malone drew back a little but did not lose sight of the three men for, as they stood at the front door, he could watch them in the mirror that, attached to the window frame outside, was adjusted so that the door and steps were fully visible.

It was a precaution that had served Malone well on occasions when his visitor had been unwelcome and, in some cases, had come with the pleasant intention of shooting him if he could get a chance to sling a gun.

But there was nothing of that intent about this trio. They had obviously come upon some matter that was worrying them for, while one put his finger to the bell, the other two shifted restlessly and kept glancing impatiently at the door.

Malone could hear his manservant going along the hall. By the time Baxter was ushering the visitors into the sitting-room, Malone was seated at his desk reading a letter.

It was the one he took to be the eldest of the trio, a short, stocky man with clean-shaven intellectual face and eye-glasses who introduced himself and his companions.

"My name is Crabbe, Mr. Malone," he said in an oddly deep voice as he passed the famous detective a card. "I am, as you will see by my card, a solicitor and my two brothers have come with me. This," and he indicated the other one of professional appearance, "is my brother Henry, who is an architect. And this," here he waved towards the youngest, who seemed none too anxious to come under Malone's scrutiny, "is my brother Gerald."

Malone acknowledged the introductions, noting that the first name of the speaker was "James." So, here he had before him, three gentlemen of the name of Crabbe—James, solicitor; Henry, architect; and Gerald, of no stated calling.

"Please sit down, gentlemen. Am I to take it that you are some kin of the man who was found murdered at Mitcham?"

"You have seen about that in the papers, then, Mr. Malone?" said James Crabbe as he dropped into a chair.

"Yes. And, of course, the name is none too common."

"Exactly. Well, you have guessed right. We are or were nephews of Jacob Crabbe and it is because a very unpleasant situation has arisen in connection with that affair that we have come to lay the matter before you. I may say that my own profession has given me an opportunity to watch some of your cases and for that reason I thought we could not do better than get your opinion. The situation is bad and, indeed, I should not be surprised if we had been followed here by plainclothes officers. To be frank, all of us appear to be under some sort of suspicion regarding the murder of our uncle and my brother, Gerald, is, we fear, in imminent danger of arrest."

"The papers have hinted nothing of that. They have simply made the usual statement—that Scotland Yard is in possession of valuable clues and that an arrest is expected at any moment."

"Well, in this case, I am afraid that statement is not eyewash."

"Perhaps you will let me hear what you have to say."

"I may take it, I think, that you know the facts as well as we. What I wish to lay before you is our situation in relation to police activity since yesterday."

"Let me see, the crime was discovered the night before last."

"Yes. And I had a visit at my office from the police yesterday morning. They also called upon my brother Henry. In each case they made searching inquiries regarding the whereabouts and recent movements of my brother Gerald. It was only this morning we were able to locate him and, in view of the situation, I thought we should lose no time in coming to you. I am certain that my movements have been closely shadowed since yesterday and my brother Henry says the same."

Malone nodded and reached for the big silver box that held a supply of the choice partagas cigars that he favoured. He passed these round, managing to get another good look at Gerald Crabbe as he did so. He was not yet ready to place this brother in connection with the other two or the elder brother's statement.

"Scotland Yard is very efficient," he agreed non-committally.

"But suppose you tell me the exact problem that is worrying you, that is, why your brother fears arrest."

"We fear it is to be charged with the murder of our uncle."

"That is serious. And, of course, he denies it or you would not have come to me."

For the first time Gerald Crabbe spoke and now his words came in an almost hysterical outburst.

"I'm innocent. I swear it, Mr. Malone. I've never laid a finger on the old man, though I confess I've felt like kicking him often enough. But I wasn't at the house that night."

"Then, with an alibi, you should have nothing to fear."

"That's just the trouble," put in James Crabbe, "he has no alibi."

"I don't quite understand. He must have been somewhere and it is difficult, I should say, to spend any considerable time among one's fellow-men without being seen or noted by someone. Am I permitted to ask where you were, Mr. Crabbe?"

Both James and Henry Crabbe turned to their brother.

"Tell him what you told us, Gerry."

The young man swallowed. He turned slightly and now, with the full light upon his face, Malone thought that it was a dissipated and ravaged one. It was easy enough to deduce that here was a young man who did not put a brake on his pleasures or weaknesses. And there was in it, too, plenty of indications of a quick and savage temper. But Malone did not urge him on. He waited patiently, smoking.

"I was at Newmarket most of the week," said Gerald Crabbe, at last. "I went down on Monday night for the four days' meeting but I did not last it out. I had the worst run of luck I've ever known. So, as I couldn't carry on with the bookies any longer and couldn't raise a bean on loan, I thought I'd come back to town and see what I could do here."

He paused and glanced at his two brothers as if for confirmation or encouragement. The eldest smiled thinly.

"Perhaps I had better explain to Mr. Malone that I and my brother Henry allow my youngest brother a certain amount monthly. It is understood that, under no circumstances is he to draw anything against us for anything additional.—Er— my brother Gerald has a disinclination for any calling that binds him too closely. In fact, Mr. Malone, he wastes both time and money, I am afraid, but we have never believed in dictating one to the other beyond a certain point."

Lawrence Malone could read the meaning of that statement. It revealed that, while the two elder brothers might disapprove strongly of the younger's way of life, they had for him an affection that survived these shortcomings. In other words, Gerald Crabbe was a waster, as the saying goes, but the other two were "soft" enough to pay him an allowance out of their own (presumably) substantial incomes that enabled him to continue his useless way. It is a condition of things not unusual in families where the bond of affection is knit tightly.

Malone covered the pause with a smile, Gerald Crabbe went on with his statement.

"I wouldn't have gone to my brothers for a loan," he said. "They have always been far too decent to me, anyway. But I thought I might raise the wind in one or two other directions and I was anxious to do so before to-day for the meeting at Kempton Park. I know a dead certainty that is running in the three-thirty."

For a few moments the trait in his character that made him an inveterate gambler was uppermost to the exclusion of everything else. His eyes shone and his fingers snapped nervously as his mind rested on the "dead cert" that was running this same day. The other two brothers looked at him disapprovingly; Lawrence Malone smiled cynically. He had seen something of "dead certs" in his own reckless days.

But not even that great passion could prevail for long against the other emotion that gripped him. Now, as Malone saw a hunted look come into his eyes, he suddenly realised that Gerald Crabbe was afraid, mortally afraid about something. If he was innocent of the crime that was threatening to be laid at his door why should he be afraid?

His voice was husky and faltering as he finished his statement in a rush of words.

"I'd better tell you at once that I intended going down to Mitcham to see my uncle. I didn't think it would be much use but I was desperate and made up my mind to take a chance. Well, I phoned my brother James about five o'clock from Liverpool Street, then I took a Number 11 bus to Victoria Street Station with the intention of catching a train for Mitcham round about six o'clock. Well, I didn't get one until after seven."

"Why?"

It was Malone who shot the question at him.

"To tell you the truth, I ran into a bunch of fellows I knew at Victoria Station and went into the bar with them. We were there until seven or so. There was one of them from whom I thought I might raise a bit but it was no go. Then I travelled on to Mitcham and arrived there about twenty minutes to eight."

"So you were in Mitcham on the same evening as the murder and round about the time at which it is said to occur?"

"Yes."

"But not at your uncle's house?"

"No. I swear I didn't go as far as the door."

"Why not? You say you went there for the sole purpose of trying to see him."

"I lost my nerve. If I hadn't had a good deal to drink coming up from Newmarket I don't suppose I'd have got the idea of going to see him. The last time I was there we had the devil's own row and he told me never to come to the house again. But we'd had lots of rows before."

"But how did you spend your time in Mitcham?"

"I'll explain. Back at Victoria I was glad to run into the bunch of fellows I knew. I was already funking the idea but a few more rounds of drinks made me more determined than ever to carry on. When I came out of the station at Mitcham I made for the first pub and had a couple more drinks. Then I walked in the direction of Sutton Road, where my uncle lived. I must have been walking about in that neighbourhood for the better part of an hour trying to make up my mind to enter the gate, but I was funking it worse than ever, with the upshot that I came away without getting within a hundred yards of the place."

"So, from the time you left the public house outside Mitcham Station until you returned to the station there is no one to account for your movements?"

"Not a soul."

"Did you meet anyone?"

"I passed one or two persons, but it was drizzling and it wasn't possible to see clearly. I don't suppose I was noticed particularly."

"What about the people at the public house?"

"The barmaid might remember that I had a couple of drinks round about eight o'clock and again a little before nine. But that doesn't cover the intervening time, and my brothers say that the murder could have been committed during that period. That's why my alibi isn't any good."

"But, if you are innocent, then you can rely on your statement being given full consideration and, of course, if the guilty person is found there will be all you need."

It was here that James Crabbe, the eldest of the brothers, intervened.

"That isn't the chief danger, Mr. Malone," he said slowly. "That isn't why I decided that we must come on and see you without delay."

"What is the reason then?"

"This. When my brother was drinking with those fellows at Victoria he made a statement which can be construed most damnably against him."

"Ah! What was it?"

"Tell him the exact words, Gerald."

"As far as I can remember, Mr. Malone, I said that I was going down to Mitcham to strike my old wolf of an uncle for a loan and if he refused me I'd take it out of his hide. They— they will remember that when they realise my connection with the murdered man."

CHAPTER FOUR

Confirmation of this fear was to come sooner than even Lawrence Malone anticipated; and Malone knew better than anyone present how ruthless and how fast the police mill can grind.

He had already realised that a man of the profession and experience of James Crabbe would not have sought his advice unless there was something that filled him with grave uneasiness. Now he knew what it was.

But Malone had not anticipated that this something would turn out to be as serious as it undoubtedly was. Baldly put, the situation resolved itself into a problem which might or might not be found possible of solution if Gerald Crabbe was innocent.

If he was innocent.

There was the rub. The facts were ominous to say the least. It was stated in the information which the police had issued to the press that Jacob Crabbe had been murdered somewhere about eight o'clock on the Thursday evening.

They had not allowed any hint to appear of suspicions against the nephews. But Malone knew now that they must have been working on this from the first.

Who, then, had first given the police information that had caused them to turn their attention in this direction?

Then there was Gerald Crabbe's statement. By this he acknowledged that he had been at Mitcham at the time the murder must have been done and he could provide no alibi for the vital period of time.

Was he telling the truth? Or was it that, faced by a terrible dilemma, he was being guided along this line of statement by his eldest brother who, with his knowledge of the law, realised that, if he were guilty, his only hope was to admit some of what must come out and trust to a jury to give him the benefit of any doubt about the rest?

Then there was the most damning part of all. He had mixed with acquaintances before going down to Mitcham. Flushed with drink and, Malone could guess, with his anxiety to raise money, he had made foolish statements which, in view of what had followed, would be only too well remembered.

If he was guilty, why had he been brought to him (Lawrence Malone)? James Crabbe must know that Malone would have nothing to do with any case which meant helping a murderer to evade the consequences of his deed. If such were the case he would find Malone's anger a most unpleasant thing to deal with.

But, on the other hand, if he were innocent of the murder— if he were, in fact, an unfortunate victim of circumstances through his own foolish actions and loosely-guarded tongue, then how could the truth be discovered?

Malone looked the three brothers straight in the eye, one after the other, bringing his gaze back to rest on the eldest.

"What do you wish me to do?" he asked curtly.

"Save my brother," was the prompt reply.

"I should have to be convinced of his innocence."

"Mr. Malone, I give you my word of honour that I should not waste your time unless I knew that my brother was innocent. I have been into this thing with him. He has convinced me in a way that I know is beyond doubt. I ask you to take no brief for his foolish indiscretions, but I do ask you to find the person who did murder my uncle."

"You said when you first spoke that you had been interviewed by the police and that your brother was already in danger of being arrested. What caused the police to turn their attention in his direction so soon?"

"That confounded housekeeper must have done it."

"Housekeeper—I think I must have further information on this point."

It was at this moment that Malone happened to glance towards the window. Beyond the glass he could see the telltale mirror which reflected the front door and steps. The angle of vision was perfect from where he sat.

And, just mounting the steps, he saw Detective-Inspector Latham of Scotland Yard accompanied by two plainclothes officers.

He watched until he saw Latham lift his hand to the bell. Then he rose swiftly.

"It looks as though your fears were well founded," he said quietly. "Inspector Latham is at the front door with two officers. You understand, if he has followed you here and demands the person of one or all of you, I cannot refuse to let him do his duty."

Gerald Crabbe had turned as white as chalk. His hands gripped the arms of his chair and he gazed at Malone as if hypnotised. Henry

Crabbe was showing signs or agitation almost as acute. Only James Crabbe managed to keep his composure.

"We quite understand, Mr. Malone. But are we to take it that you cannot or will not help us?"

"Not at all. I cannot give you a definite decision until I know more, but my inclination at the moment is to accept the commission. In the meantime I am going to ask you all to step into an adjoining room and wait there. I shall hear what Inspector Latham has to say."

The bell could be heard ringing in the hall. Malone crossed to a door and opened it, ushering his three visitors into a small smoking-room. Then he took swift note that they had carried their cigars with them, dumped the ashes from two trays into one, pushed the chairs back and was at his desk puffing away at his own cigar when his man ushered in Latham. He was alone, so Malone assumed that he had left the two plainclothes men out in the hall.

He greeted the Scotland Yard man affably.

"Well, well, if it isn't friend Latham looking as determined as if he expected to find me hoarding Irish Sweep tickets. Sit down and take a cigar."

Latham, who had a peculiar weakness for Malone's partagas, permitted himself a brief smile and, when Malone pushed the silver box of cigars across, "absent-mindedly" helped himself to half a dozen.

But, when that was lit, he glared at Malone frowningly.

"Where are they?" he demanded curtly. "None of your jiggery-pokery now, Malone. I want them."

"You've just taken a half-dozen of them," returned Malone blandly.

Latham flushed but held his ground.

"You are trying jiggery-pokery and I won't have it. You know what I want. Where are they?"

"My dear fellow, will you please be more explicit?" asked Malone plaintively.

"You know well enough what I mean. I want the Crabbes. They came here I know. My men followed them and saw them enter. And they haven't come out. Their car is still at the kerb."

"That is rather a giveaway, isn't it? Well, assuming for the sake of argument that you want me to hand over three persons of the name of Crabbe, and I haven't acknowledged yet that they are here, why do you want them?"

"Murder, Malone, murder and don't waste time quibbling."

"Dear me, murder is serious. Do you wish to arrest all three on the charge. They must have been doing it wholesale."

"Listen, Malone. I have a warrant for the arrest of one of them, Gerald Crabbe, on a charge of murder. I am to use my discretion whether I arrest the other two as accomplices or not. I intend taking all three along to the Yard to get their statements. Now you know, so produce them."

"All right, old man, keep your shirt on. They are safe enough. I should inform you, however, that I have been formally retained to look after their interests, so it might make filings pleasant for both of us if you would let me know just why you are so definite about Gerald Crabbe."

"I'm not prepared to go into details now, Malone, but I don't mind telling you that we've got the goods on him. There's no mystery about this job. It's dead open-and-shut. I don't know why they've come to you or what they think you can do for them. You are only wasting your time."

"Well, if I am disposed to do so, I take it you will not place any obstacles in my way. To be quite frank with you, Latham, I'd like to go out to the scene of the crime and have a look round."

"You are perfectly welcome to do so, but, I warn you, all you will find is something that will help to tighten the noose round that bird's neck."

Malone smiled crookedly.

"All right, but I shall have to do something to justify my foe."

"Get all you can, old man, for he won't be able to pay anyone anything much longer. And now, hand them over."

"Wait here."

Malone rose and crossed the room. Latham would have liked to follow him but knew that Malone would not stand for that. In any other case, the man from Scotland Yard would have demanded and insisted that there be no delay at all, but he knew that if Lawrence Malone said he would hand over the persons he wanted, he would do so. So he sat and chewed on the end of one of Malone's partagas while, in the other room, the detective was speaking in low tones to the three brothers.

"There is no help for it," he was telling James Crabbe. "Inspector

Latham is determined to arrest your youngest brother and to take you along to Scotland Yard in order to get a statement. Frankly, you stand a good chance of being arrested there as accessories to the crime with which your brother is to be charged."

"Can you do nothing?"

"I am helpless at the moment to prevent police action. Nor would I do so. But I have told you that I accept the commission and I shall get to work immediately to see what can be done. My best advice to you is to accept things as they come without protest. You two," here he indicated James and Henry Crabbe, "might have a chance of bail. But do not make things too difficult. You must trust me to do all that is possible."

"We will be guided entirely by you, Mr. Malone."

"There is just one thing then that l shall require before we go out to Inspector Latham."

"What is that? Money? I can write you a cheque now."

"Not money. I ask no fee at present. That will depend, entirely on the result of my efforts. It is something far more important to me than a fee. It is a definite statement by your brother, Gerald Crabbe, that he is innocent."

He turned suddenly and gazed straight into the eyes of the youngest brother.

"Well?" he asked curtly.

Gerald Crabbe had recovered some of his composure after the first shock of impending arrest. He met Malone's eyes squarely enough at first but, under that deliberate stare, his own faltered at last.

"I—I am innocent. I swear it," he blurted out.

Even then Malone could not discard the niggling doubt that persisted. The evidence against Gerald Crabbe was so condemning— his alibi so feeble.

It was more the assurance of the eldest brother, James Crabbe, that influenced him more than anything else to carry on—that and, perhaps, a perfectly natural desire to discover if the case was as completely open-and-shut as Latham insisted.

For Malone was not forgetting that, in the few details contained in the papers, it had been said that the murdered man had been found in a room where both windows and door were locked on the inside. And Malone did not picture Gerald Crabbe as possessing sufficient intellectual cunning to carry out a murder along such subtle lines.

He did not press the matter further then. He merely nodded in response to Gerald Crabbe's words and, turning, opened the door.

Then, with an ironic glance at Inspector Latham, he surrendered the three brothers into his charge.

CHAPTER FIVE

Lawrence Malone was engaged for a very short time upon what was to gain wide notoriety as the Mitcham Murder before he realised that he was up against something far more complicated and more carefully planned than at first appeared.

The difference between his approach to the problem and that of Inspector Latham was in the matter of conviction.

Almost immediately after his arrival upon the scene, Latham had heard the statement of the housekeeper. This, although coloured by her obvious dislike or, rather, hatred of the nephews, was one that could not be ignored.

A circumstance that occurred soon after his return to Scotland Yard clinched the matter in Latham's mind. This was the receipt of an anonymous letter.

Now, in the ordinary course of events, right-thinking people pay no attention to such letters, for they are usually penned by cowardly persons with malicious intent. But at Scotland Yard nothing is discarded without being carefully analysed and its possible importance gauged.

The writer was obviously one who had read about the Mitcham murder in the papers and who had had no difficulty in connecting the name with that of Gerald Crabbe. The letter ran as follows:

"Gerald Crabbe, a nephew of the man who was murdered at Mitcham, can tell you something about it. There are witnesses who heard him threaten to do his uncle in. This was at Victoria Station early the same evening as the murder, and he was on his way to Mitcham then.

"(Signed) ONE WHO OVERHEARD."

If it wasn't true, it was a most vicious communication. If it was true, then there was a very definite question that Inspector Latham wanted to ask Gerald Crabbe.

It did not take long to pick up his trail. The chase began with locating James and Henry Crabbe and then, through them, finding the other brother.

But the three made a move to see Lawrence Malone before Latham had his warrant ready. Hence their brief respite before he arrived at Malone's house to demand their surrender. But they had not been out of sight of Latham's watchdogs for a single moment.

So convinced, therefore, was Latham that Gerald Crabbe was the man he wanted and that his two brothers were very probably accessories both before and after the fact, that he entirely lost sight of details surrounding the murder that otherwise he might have examined more closely.

These were the locked conditions of windows and doors as well as other channels of enquiry which might yield something of value.

Malone, not being entirely convinced one way or the other (though he was bound, for the moment, to give his client the benefit of any doubt) was able to keep a more open mind.

To him, the case was a problem that must be tackled from every possible angle with the object of finding some clue which might suggest a culprit different from Gerald Crabbe.

In this he was bound to weigh Gerald Crabbe's mental capacity. Was he capable of planning and carrying out a crime that needed so much attention to detail?

Let it be supposed that, for some time past, he had secretly resolved to kill his uncle and get away with what money he might find, he, or anyone carrying out the murder as it had been done, would require to know certain details. That was evident from the conditions in which things had been found.

Unquestionably, Gerald Crabbe would know when to find his uncle at home. He would know that he seldom left the house. He would also know on what evening or days the housekeeper and maid would be absent. This knowledge must have been acquired from his frequent visits to the house and, as for that, it would be known to James and Henry Crabbe as well.

But at this point another question arose in Malone's mind. Was Gerald Crabbe mentally capable of planning a crime in such fashion? It needed a subtle and agile mind to conceive and carry out the murder of Jacob Crabbe and, somehow, Malone did not picture Gerald Crabbe as possessing those qualities. Still, he conceded, that one never knew.

Assuming, however, that Gerald Crabbe might have done so, either alone or with assistance, what did he expect to gain? He surely could not have counted on securing any great sum of ready money, for the available evidence seemed to show that the contents of the safe were intact. (Malone realised, of course, that the safe might have been opened and closed by someone who knew the combination and who might have taken only some particular document).

Nevertheless, the list which Inspector Latham had permitted him to see showed a large sum in banknotes which no ordinary thief would be fool enough to leave behind unless driven for time; and all the earmarks of the murder seemed to show that no such pressure had existed.

Then, assuming that Gerald Crabbe might have been the murderer, what might have been his motive? The will? That was unsigned. Did he kill his uncle because he knew the will was unsigned and thus was determined that it never should receive his signature? If so, he would only be able to share as next-of-kin providing he was never accused of the murder. Likewise, his two brothers would be debarred, for a recent High Court ruling had lain it down that no close kin of a murderer could share in any benefit resulting from such murder. There was certainly a line of suggestion there but it was so far obscure.

Another thing that struck Malone forcibly. He believed that the hand that had killed Jacob Crabbe had belonged to someone whom he knew intimately, for Crabbe was a man whom few persons could approach and he would only remain with his back to such person if he felt he had nothing to fear from such approach. Therefore he put it down that the murderer had been known to Jacob Crabbe.

But Gerald Crabbe was not the only person who fulfilled those conditions. Both the housekeeper and the maid qualified; likewise James and Henry Crabbe and, for that matter, some old gentleman along the street with whom the dead man had been on some sort of friendly terms.

Malone soon decided that the maid could be eliminated. She was an honest but stupid girl, quite incapable of a deed requiring such decision of character. But he did not dismiss the housekeeper from his calculations. She had the necessary strength of character to devise such a plan if, perhaps, not the requisite physical strength to carry it out, though Malone believed a strong woman could have struck that blow. That possibility, however, by no means made Mrs. Deason a murderess.

Besides, by her own showing, she was to have married Jacob Crabbe. Was it likely, then, that she would murder the person from whom she expected to receive such social and financial benefits?

On the other hand, did she know that Crabbe's will was unsigned? Malone did not think so. If she had known then she must have realised that Crabbe's death would be disastrous to her.

But it was possible that Crabbe had lied to her about that. He may have told her the will was signed in order to keep her from pestering him. Such lies have been told before and Malone did not think Crabbe was the sort to quibble at such a thing if it suited his purpose. Moreover, since his interview with the housekeeper, he could believe that the old man had become so entangled that he was completely under her thumb and he thought it possible that the question of marriage had originated with her rather than with him.

Against all this, however, there was something that seemed to eliminate Mrs. Deason as a suspect as completely as the maid. This was her alibi for that evening. It seemed unassailable.

From the time she left the house on the fatal evening until she returned about ten, her movements were vouched for by the invalid sister whom she had gone to visit. This sister lived in another part of Mitcham and had been interviewed personally by Inspector Latham. Latham was perfectly satisfied with her statement.

As for the maid, it had been confirmed that, as she stated, she had gone to the cinema with her "young man." He, as having a sort of secondary connection with the household, had been identified as a perfectly respectable grocer's assistant.

Some of these reflections Malone was not able to consider fully until after his first visit to the house of the murder. In fact, it was not even then that he was able to array them for examination, for immediately following that, there occurred an incident so strange that Malone found it difficult to put it down as what appeared to be—just an unfortunate accident. In order to understand just how this came about and why, later, it was to form a very strong link in the chain of evidence which Malone was forging, it is necessary to take his movements in sequence.

It was just on mid-day when Inspector Latham left Malone's house with the three Crabbe brothers. Following their departure, Malone returned to the work which had been interrupted by their visit and was busy with this until Baxter served lunch.

It was a little after two when he rang up Scotland Yard to learn that a definite charge of murder had been filed against Gerald Crabbe and that, for the time being, the other two brothers were being held as material witnesses. He also learned that the inquest on the body of Jacob Crabbe would take place the following morning at eleven o'clock.

With this much to go on, Malone drove to Mitcham.

The group of morbidly inclined people that had hung about the house for the first day or so following the murder had now disappeared. The reporters were giving the thing a rest at this end owing to the police statement that an arrest had been made. There was no constable on duty outside, but a man in uniform opened the door to Malone and, when he had seen Malone's permit from Scotland Yard, admitted him somewhat dubiously.

Malone met the stiffness with perfect good humour. He was used to this attitude which usually altered materially before his contact with such persons was finished.

"Who is in the house?" he asked crisply.

"The housekeeper and the maid, sir, but I don't know—"

"I know what you are going to say," Malone interrupted him. "You need not be alarmed that I intend questioning you. If I have any question to put to the police I shall wait until your own inspector comes along. But I fancy I shall want a word with the housekeeper. Firstly, however, I wish to have a look at the room where the crime was committed. Where is the body?"

"The room you want, sir, is that door on the right. The body has been taken to a bedroom upstairs."

Malone nodded and started down the hall. As he went along he noted that it was badly lit, the lower end being only vaguely outlined in the gloom. It was not so dim, however, that, as he went along quietly, he did not see the door of a room on the left being closed very gently.

Someone had witnessed his visit and must have been listening to what passed between him and the constable. Who was it— the housekeeper or the maid?

He was inclined to throw the door open suddenly and surprise whoever might be on the other side, but he did not wish to show his knowledge then, so turned and pushed open the door of the study that, owing to the broken lock, hung slightly ajar.

Malone closed the door and stood gazing about the room. At first, his eyes took in the main features of the apartment, its furniture, the arrangement, the untidy state and the lighting conditions.

Not until the whole layout was stamped in his mind so thoroughly that he could have moved about blindfolded did he advance towards the desk and seat himself in the chair that had been occupied by the dead man when he was struck down.

He found that, now his back was towards the door and that he faced the two windows, one being a little to the right of his direct line of vision, the other to the left. They looked out upon the garden which stretched to a nearby high hedge that separated the place from its neighbour.

For artificial lighting, there was an electric desk lamp and a ceiling bulb. That was all.

Malone rose. His intention now was to reconstruct the conditions as nearly as possible as they must have been when the crime was committed. He walked to the door in order to examine the key that, he understood, had been on the inside at the time, but found that it was missing. He concluded that it had been taken away by Inspector Latham and was just turning back to extend his examination to the locks of the windows when, suddenly, the floor seemed to lift beneath his feet, then followed with the violent roar and heavy concussion of an appalling explosion that was so close it appeared to be under the very foundations.

CHAPTER SIX

Malone was still deaf from the violent assault upon his eardrums when the rocking of the house ceased.

He had been through a disastrous earthquake once in Central America and his present sensation was exactly as he had experienced then with the exception that, during the earthquake, there had been no such terrible explosion.

He recovered quickly and dragged the door open. Racing along the hall he saw that the front door was wide and then discovered that this was because it had been blown clean inwards. Then he saw the front garden, the hedge and the gate. It was exactly as if a bomb had dropped in the street outside.

He found the constable sprawled half-unconscious beneath the wreckage of the front door. The fellow was groaning, but Malone did not stop now to aid him. He continued through the aperture that had been the front door and found the steps partially blown away. He leaped to the ground and ran down the path to the gate. Then, as he reached it, he drew up, dumbfounded at the sight that met his eyes.

Here, directly in front of him, was, he knew, the spot where the worst of the explosion had expended its force. The pavement and roadway showed a gaping hole big enough to swallow a taxicab and this was exactly the spot where, a few minutes before, Malone's glistening new sports car had stood. But of the car there was now not the slightest sign. It had vanished as if it had never been.

The fence and hedging right along on each side were blown flat. Windows on the opposite side of the street had been shattered and, a little way along to the left, was some debris that, later, Malone found was the wreckage of what had been a coal dray. There had been a driver and a horse but, like his car, they had been blown to bits.

The street was filling with terrified people, each asking the other what had happened. A woman in the near distance was screaming hysterically and a man's deep bass could be heard trying to silence her. But it was from a little old man that Malone got his first clue as to what had actually occurred. He found a little later that this individual was the same neighbour who had been summoned by the housekeeper on the night Jacob Crabbe was murdered.

"I saw it, I saw it," he croaked to Malone. "I was just coming down the steps of my house when it happened."

"What did you see, sir?"

"There was a car here, a brand new red car it was. And there was a coal cart just there." Here he waved his arm towards the debris that Malone had already seen. "The driver he wanted to pull in close to the kerb, so he came along and began to push the car."

"Push the car!" exclaimed Malone. "But it was my car and the handbrake was on."

"He loosened the brake. I saw it all, I tell you. Then he began to push the car along and—whoof! it came just like that. I was almost knocked down but I saw it all. The car and the man vanished just as if they'd never been there. It's a wonder the whole street isn't in ruins. You say it was your car. Now why did it go up like that?"

"I don't know, I don't know," rejoined Malone thoughtfully. "Do you mind, sir, if I ask you a question or two?"

"Not at all, not at all."

"You say the explosion occurred just as the man from the coal dray was pushing my car along?"

"Yes, I've just told you, haven't I?"

"And that the explosion came from somewhere in the close vicinity of the car?"

"From inside the car, I should say. I tell you the whole car just went into nothing."

Suddenly the old man seemed to regard Malone in a new light.

"Your car, you say? Then you are responsible for all this damage and the death of that man, too. You must have had some explosive in that car of yours."

Malone was saved any reply that might have given the other cause for further charges by the appearance of a constable running up the road. The sight of the man recalled to Malone's mind the wounded officer he had left in the hall. And, at this same moment, he saw two women running down the path from the house he had just left.

One, he knew instinctively, must be the housekeeper; the other he had no difficulty in placing as the maid.

They drew up at the gate and he noticed that the old gentleman who affirmed he had witnessed the explosion greeted the housekeeper as if he knew her. Then it dawned on Malone that the old fellow must be the neighbour who had been called in on the night of the murder.

Next moment the constable arrived. Malone would have re-entered the gate but felt his arm tugged.

"You wait here," he heard the old fellow saying. "You can tell the constable about the car."

Malone grew suddenly angry. He had no wish to disclose his identity before any collection of strangers, but neither did he intend to be catechised in the street about a matter that was, to him, one of growing and sinister mystery.

He was remembering that the explosion had come from his car, and that it had occurred as soon as the car had been put in motion. Suppose no passing drayman had wished to get his cart in against the kerb where his car was occupying space and had pushed it along a little? What then? It was a thousand to one on that the car would have been left untouched until he, Malone, stepped in and drove off. And then? He would have been completely annihilated just as the coal man had vanished.

There had been nothing of an explosive nature in the car when he drove out from London or when he had parked it at the kerb. If the story told by the old gentleman was true, then an explosive of a most violent and destructive nature had been placed somewhere in the car during the brief period of his absence inside the house. With what purpose? It looked uncommonly ugly to Malone, as though it had been intended that he should be the one to start the car after the explosive had been planted and that it was a deliberate attempt to blow him into smithereens.

If this was so, then, why? Malone had lots of enemies among the criminal underworld. He never stepped among them that he didn't carry his life in his hands. But he was used to that and went prepared.

This, however, was different. No ordinary tough of the underworld had sprung this trap out here in Mitcham. To do so would have meant that his intended movements that day were known. And, until just before he left his house, he had not definitely decided to make that particular journey.

Then what? Was it possible that the thing had been devised and put into effect on the spur of the moment? Was the perpetrator someone who had not expected him on the scene but, finding him, had lost no time in attempting to eliminate him as a potential danger?

Danger in what way? What had brought him to Mitcham? The murder of Jacob Crabbe. Did someone fear that he was more danger than the police? That he might discover something that they had missed?

If so then it meant that the person who had made such reckless efforts to dispose of him must have been close at hand when he arrived, might, even now, be near.

He remembered that door that had closed so stealthily in the dimness of the hall. He wished now that he had thrown it open to discover what hand was on the other side. Whose was it? Where had the housekeeper been at the time? And the maid? And, if it came to that, what about this old fellow who was now telling the constable his version of the affair?

But, as he regarded them thoughtfully, Lawrence Malone found it difficult to believe that any one of the trio could be associated with such a dastardly outrage as had just been perpetrated in this quiet Mitcham street in the early afternoon.

The housekeeper, a quiet-looking woman of serene and respectable mien, the maid, equally respectable of appearance but utterly unequal to any prolonged or subtle mental effort, and the old gentleman of garrulous tongue, who appeared altogether too decrepit for such strenuous activities. No, the answer didn't seem to lie there. But—who had closed that door?

By now, the constable was gazing at Malone in a suspiciously inquiring way. Malone shrugged.

"I was inside this house when the explosion occurred," he said curtly. "It is true, as this gentleman says, that my car has disappeared. I am quite willing to make a statement later, but, at the moment, I think we are needed inside the house. Your colleague there was injured when the door blew in. And here, for your private information, is something that will explain my presence here."

The constable's manner altered magically when he saw the permit that had been issued by Scotland Yard. He, unlike his colleague, had personal knowledge of the association that existed between the famous detective and the Yard. He saluted smartly.

"I should be glad of anything you can tell me, sir. And I'd better come into the house with you. I can use the telephone. I was on duty here yesterday."

Malone nodded and led the way up the path. He noticed that the housekeeper followed, with the maid at her heels, while the old fellow stared after them agape.

But Malone's mind was not occupied now with that individual's wordy meanderings. He was concentrating every faculty upon the amazing problem that faced him.

Within this house, he told himself, lay the answer to the riddle. Gerald Crabbe could not be accused of the latest outrage. He was safe in the hands of the police.

The culprit had been close to him within a few minutes. Was it the same who had done the murder? Or was there some entirely different answer to the question?

He stood at the front door and peered down the hall. The gloom seemed to mock him. Yet beyond that obscurity, beyond the door that had closed so stealthily, he believed his answer lay. But he believed even more strongly that he would find a tortuous and perilous path to trace before he reached the end.

He was right, deadly right.

CHAPTER SEVEN

A man and a woman talked together in a small, very neat and clean bedroom.

The woman was in bed and her face displayed the pallor of the chronic invalid.

The man was well dressed in a loose-fitting suit of dark blue serge. He sat close to the bed so that, speaking in low tones, their voices were no more than a low murmur.

It was evening. Outside in the quiet road a fine drizzle made the pavements wet and glistening beneath the street lamps.

The woman seemed concerned about the matter which was the subject of their talk for, from time to time, she would clutch at the well-shaped brown hand of the other and her fingers would work convulsively. The man seemed to be trying to soothe her.

"I tell you it is going to be all right," he kept reassuring her. "No one could have anticipated that the old fool was lying all the time. You leave things to me, my dear. I've cracked tougher nuts before and I'll crack this one."

"But I hate to think of you working without me. If this cursed back of mine didn't keep me tied to this bed I could be of some use."

A spasm of pain crossed the face of the other.

"Don't. You wouldn't be there if it hadn't been for my carelessness. We've got to get you right again and it takes money to pay the medical sharks. If that old fool hadn't been lying everything would have been jake. But never mind. I'll settle matters to-night."

"Will it be necessary to take further risks?"

"If you mean will I have to go to extremes, no. That is, not unless that nosey detective is hanging about. But I don't think he will return in a hurry. It was just bad luck that he wasn't in the car when it went to pieces. If that interfering coalman hadn't come along just then the thing would have worked like a charm."

"But the police—what about the other?"

"There's nothing to worry about. It will take more than Scotland Yard or Lawrence Malone to discover the truth of that job. Besides, they've got the Crabbes in hand and they can't do anything but pin it on to one of them. They've got too much to think about to be any danger to us."

"That old devil—I wish you'd known before."

"Well, when he lied to Clara Deason about the signing of that will he didn't know what he had to deal with. He knows now. And so will that detective if he pokes about any more."

"Just the same, I'm worried about to-night. It seems an awful risk. I wish I could come along and give you a hand."

"I tell you, it will be as easy as cutting butter; and it's our last chance. To think that the stuff was there all the time and I never knew it. He wasn't such an old fool as Clara Deason took him for. He was cunning all right. But the inquest is to-morrow and after that the stuff will be removed. It's tonight or never. And we've got to have the stuff. I'm not going to pass it up after all the time we've spent on, the job—two years or more."

"What time will you go?"

"About midnight. There will be only one constable on duty but he won't give any trouble. There will be another one out in the road but he won't hear anything. I can get in and out without a hitch. And once I reach that safe it won't take me five minutes to clean it out. The police didn't know that Clara Deason was listening when they went through the list. There's a good few thousands there that can be realised immediately and a lot more that can be put through—you know who."

"All the same, I wish I could go along if only to keep watch. It's the devil being so useless."

Which, on the face of it, seemed a remarkable expression from one whose appearance and invalid condition seemed so alien to the subject under discussion.

"Don't talk that way. You wouldn't be where you are if I hadn't bungled that other job. As soon as I get my hands on that stuff to-night we will wait until things are quiet and then we'll fade away. I've got everything planned,"

"All right, I'll not worry. But take care of yourself."

The other nodded and rose. From beneath the bed he pulled a small steel uniform box such as are used by officers on foreign service. He unlocked this and, after rummaging about for a few moments, brought out some well-worn garments, a pair of black canvas "sneakers" or rubber-soled shoes, a small but weighty "life-preserver," a gun, a small electric torch and a delicately fashioned microphone.

He carried these into another room and, during his absence, the woman in the bed thrust her hand under the pillow and brought out a small automatic pistol with a peculiar-looking circular drum attached to the underside of the barrel.

She pressed a catch so that the drum came away completely, then she gave each side a contrariwise twist so that the drum itself came in half, revealing that the interior was filled by a circular spring arrangement that was packed with small cartridges.

A count would have shown that the drum held sixty such missiles and with the additional carrying capacity of the clip in the butt which held fourteen cartridges plus a single one in the breech, there was a total of seventy-five bullets which could either be discharged one at a time or sent spitting out in a continuous stream of death at amazing speed. It was one of the most vicious weapons ever devised for the hand of a criminal smaller and of less holding capacity than a Thompson sub-machine-gun, but quite as effective in its speed and range and far easier to carry.

The woman in the bed worked the sliding mechanism back and forth until she was satisfied that every part was smoothly perfect. Next she examined the clip, snapped it into place and slid the automatic pick-up back and forth once so as to throw a cartridge into the breech. From a supply beneath the pillow she took a single cartridge which she pressed into the clip in order to fill it to full capacity, then she fitted the drum together and slipped it into place beneath the barrel. When she had finished she laid the gun on the coverlet beside her, a terrible weapon of death gleaming dully blue beneath the light.

She seemed to keep a small storehouse of objects beneath the pillow for now she drew out a cigarette case and, lighting a tube, lay back smoking while she waited.

In about a quarter of an hour the door to the adjoining room opened and a person of very different appearance from the well-dressed individual in blue slipped into the room.

Well-worn dark flannels replaced the blue serge, a soiled and ragged sweater with a huge collar covered the body and neck beneath the coat, a greasy cap was pulled well down over the head and the black, rubber-soled shoes replaced the well polished black shoes. The one who had left the room had appeared to be a person of quiet prosperity, the one who returned looked an out-and-out thug.

The woman in the bed smiled approvingly.

"You'll do," she said in a voice that was strangely eager. "But I do wish I was going, too."

"Never mind, old thing, you'll be coming along next time. Give me the gun."

The woman in the bed passed it up. The other scarcely glanced at it. There was no need after it had been through the expert fingers that had just tested it.

"You'll be taking awful chances if you use it," she said.

"I won't throw it out unless I have to. The other should be enough but, if anything should break, I'll leave something behind all right. Now I'll be getting along. There's just time to do it by the route I've planned."

The woman in the bed expressed no further caution or regrets. She simply nodded and smiled.

"Well, good hunting."

Then the other was gone. She listened to the soft footfall that went down the stairs, waited for the subdued noise of the closing front door that was followed by a low double whistle. Then there was silence.

CHAPTER EIGHT

Constable Henry Tew yawned in boredom.

He was fed up sitting alone in a house that had only a corpse for company. It wasn't as if he could have eased the boredom with a cigarette. He was denied that consolation for he was a non-smoker.

Nor could he walk down the short path to the street and have an occasional word with the constable on special duty there. He had strict orders to remain where he was, and Constable Tew was a man who obeyed instructions from his superiors.

While he did not question the wisdom of these same superiors he thought, privily, that his presence in the house was unnecessary. A corpse was a corpse and, in these days, no one wanted to steal such a thing.

As a matter of fact, Constable Tew was somewhat muddled in his honest mind about the whole mystery of the place. There was, first, the murder of the old fellow who had lived here. He told himself that the papers and the public, who were so ready to criticise the police, couldn't ask for quicker action than had been displayed on this occasion. Within a few hours of the crime, the murderer had been taken into custody and he felt that, in some way, the credit of that was reflected from Scotland Yard right down through the Mitcham police to himself.

He was not so clear about the strange explosion that had taken place outside the house that afternoon. No one seemed to know yet what it was all about or how it had been caused.

It was not known definitely how many persons might have been died at the time. There was evidence that a coal-cart had been demolished and the driver blown to pieces. This had actually been witnessed by an old gentleman who lived close at hand.

Then there had been talk that the explosion had come from a car that had been standing at the kerb at the time. The same old gentleman made that statement. But there wasn't anything but a hole in the ground to show whether a car had been there or not.

On the other hand, it seemed that this might be so for no less a person than Lawrence Malone, the famous detective had informed the police that he had left his car at the kerb that he believed it was there when the explosion took place and that it had vanished utterly.

Other neighbours had added their bits of evidence, real and

imagined, to those statements, but the police were by no means clear yet as to just what had taken place. The street was roped off, was under guard and would remain so until after the inquest.

Tew didn't know why this should be connected in any way with the murder. In fact, Inspector Garthwaite had said in his hearing that he agreed with Malone that it was probably an unsuccessful attempt upon his life but regarded it as one that might have occurred at any other point in London, he believed that enemies must have been trailing Malone for days and had seized this opportunity as the most favourable.

The constable was also puzzled as to why Lawrence Malone had been poking about the house. He was inside when the explosion took place. He had returned to the house and had remained for some time, moving about the study for an hour or more, examining the windows of that room on the outside and then interviewing the housekeeper and maid before taking himself off to the station to catch a train back to London.

At this point the constable thought kindly of the housekeeper. She and the maid had been given permission to leave the house until after the inquest and he could quite understand two women not wanting to remain in the place after what had happened even though he were there on guard.

But, before she left, the housekeeper had made some coffee and filled the vacuum flask for him so that it would be hot when he ate his supper. It stood on the floor by the chair and now, when his watch showed him it was past eleven, he thought he would break his ennui with some food.

It was round about half-past eleven when Constable Tew finished his sandwiches and about half the flask of coffee. Five minutes later he began to feel drowsy. He jerked himself upright and blinked hard in an effort to drive away the intense sleepiness that nagged him.

But, again and again, his lids fell, remaining closed a little longer each time. With a supreme effort of will he kept them open while he rose and walked down the hall.

The muscular movement seemed to drive the sleepiness away for the time being. He turned at the end and came back, admonishing himself as he did so. It was not like him to feel drowsy on duty and he had a hearty contempt for anyone who would be so overcome.

He felt all right again by the time he had done half a dozen turns of the hall, then he sat down once more and, within thirty seconds of doing so, Constable Tew was sliding to the floor limply. He rolled from his chair rather than fell and, once he was there, he lay just as he had fallen, snoring softly while the hour sped on to zero point.

Outside, another constable hunched himself beneath a tree. The drizzle was still falling. The trees and bushes were soaking. The red lanterns on the barrier that enclosed the hole in the road gleamed balefully. No one passed. Almost every house was in darkness. A light through a crack in the hastily repaired door of the house where Tew was on duty showed where his colleague also kept guard alone. But he could not slip up for a word with him. Orders were orders. He would be just as glad as Tew when this job was over.

He would have welcomed the passing of some late home-comer. Even a casual word would break the boredom. But none came. And he did not see the shadowy figure that was approaching the back of the house where Tew was on duty.

It would have been difficult to see that stealthy approach even had one known of the coming and been on the lookout for it. It was almost impossible to tell that something moved from the rear of the garden along by the thick hedge until only a few yards separated it from the back door.

There was no more than a shadow moving in shadow as it sped from the one point to the other. And, in the front hall Constable Tew could not hear the tiny tinkle of metal as a key was fitted to the lock of the back door, for he was in a profound sleep.

From the back door the cautious intruder moved through the kitchen with quiet and certain movements. A silent opening of the door leading to the dining-room was all that indicated this phase of the passage. Then the door into the front hall was swung inwards very gently and a pair of eyes peered along the hall to where Constable Tew lay in a huddle on the floor.

Three quiet steps took the intruder across the hall to the door of the study. There was no resistance there, for the door had not been secured by the police.

Constable Tew still slept while a small spotlight played on the combination of the safe in the study, and while an ear was pressed against the microphone that, by means of a rubber suction cap, clung to the face of the safe door, receiving and magnifying every soft click of the tumblers as expert fingers turned the dial this way and that.

The retreat of the intruder was as silent as his entry. But there was one difference. When the thief entered the study, the safe had contained somewhere in the neighbourhood of a hundred thousand pounds in various forms of cash and securities. When the shadow glided back through the garden the safe was empty of all but non-negotiable securities and an unsigned will.

That shadow, however, was not the only one moving stealthily abroad this night. From the moment it merged into the gloom of the garden at the back of the house, another figure had followed until, when the first was at the back door, the other was ensconced in the bushes a few yard away.

And, when the first crept out, to steal back the way it had come, the second resumed the trail to follow through the drizzle until the quarry vanished into a small house in another part of Mitcham.

CHAPTER NINE

Big Ben was chiming the hour of three when Lawrence Malone stepped out of a taxi and, pushing a banknote into the driver's hand, walked up the steps of his house.

The puzzled gaze of the man followed him. He was not yet certain whether he was being spoofed or not.

His fare had asked to be driven to this address and, after some argument, he had brought him. His voice, during the argument, had changed extraordinarily from a gruff, coarse tone to a cultured, pleasing drawl. But his garb had remained the same and, from all the knowledge he had gained of London in a good many years of driving, that taxi driver had never seen a more suspicious-looking character.

To use his own inward comment, he "wouldn't have trusted him alone with his own baby," and, certainly, the fellow looked capable of anything desperately criminal.

It might be, as he finally confessed laughingly, that he was Mr. Lawrence Malone, whose name and reputation the driver knew very well. But it wasn't until he saw the detective put a key in the lock, open the door and then, with no attempt at concealment, call out a cheery "good-night," that the driver decided it must be all right. But, even then, he was wagging his head in doubt as he drove on.

As for Malone, he did not feel half as cheery as he had allowed the other to believe. He was wet and fagged for he had had a strenuous time of it since the explosion in Mitcham the previous afternoon.

It wasn't the loss of his new car that worried him. That was fully covered by insurance and he would be put to no more trouble than a brief delay before it was replaced. Indeed, all he need do was to telephone the sales people as soon as they were open for business and explain matters to them in order to have a similar car at the kerb within the hour.

Nor was it disappointment with the result of his work during the preceding hours. On the contrary, he should have found some cause for congratulating himself upon the fact that, after drawing certain deductions from what he had found at the house of the murder, he had anticipated some events that had followed exactly as he expected.

His tiredness was due rather to depression that was born of the knowledge that the case had developed along lines utterly different from what he had looked for and was now shaping so that it seemed as though he was being driven to perform an act that he found the most unpleasant feature of his profession. What this was still remained in his own thoughts, but it was not to be long before it was revealed.

How many of those questions that he had asked himself the day before could he answer now? He believed he had found the answers to most of them and, about those which he was still uncertain, he felt he had thc cluc.

He was in agreement with Inspector Latham on one point —that the murder had been an "inside" job. But not in the same way as the inspector believed.

Latham was certain that Gerald Crabbe had done the deed and had been able to do so because of his intimate knowledge of the inside workings of the house.

Malone was equally positive now that, despite his lack of an alibi, Gerald Crabbe was innocent though he was also willing to concede that the murderer had possessed knowledge and facilities which could only be available to someone closely connected with the household.

When he re-entered the house after the explosion, Lawrence Malone had felt that the answer to the riddle lay behind the door that he had seen close so mysteriously rather than outside the front door.

But it must be confessed that he found little or nothing to give him a clue in that direction. What appeared of most value, however, and had been entirely missed by the police (due entirely, Malone was willing to acknowledge, to the rapidity with which evidence had piled up against Gerald Crabbe) was a very interesting feature about the window catches.

Even with the strength of the case against Gerald Crabbe, Malone was at a loss to understand why Latham was willing to ignore so completely the condition of door and windows at the time the body was found.

How was it that, after a knife had been plunged into the victim's back, the murderer had escaped, leaving the door and both windows locked on the inside?

It was ridiculous to suppose that this had been done to give the impression of suicide. That was impossible. It seemed to Malone rather that the murderer had created as many complications as possible so as to form a protecting screen for himself, ignoring, either thinkingly or unthinkingly, an entirely different form of risk.

But, Malone asked himself, was this danger to the murderer not minimised by the swift arrest of Gerald Crabbe? Had he counted on that to turn attention from any possible suspicion of himself and to concentrate it upon Crabbe? It certainly looked that way.

And, at first, it seemed to Malone that the mystery of the locks would remain unsolved for, where he expected to find something, nothing now existed. This was the key and lock of the door, the latter having been broken when the door was forced and the former having been taken away by someone.

Nevertheless, he turned his attention to the windows and, before actually testing the catches, studied them closely for some minutes. He also made various pressure tests upon the sashes, top and bottom, and it was while he was thus engaged he made an interesting discovery.

He found that, if one pressed against the lower sash of either, from the outside, and peered upwards while doing so, one could discern an appreciable space between the top frame of the lower sash and the lower frame of the top sash where they met.

At this point he left the room and, not choosing to reach the back through the kitchen quarters, passed through the front door and round to the side of the house by an asphalt path that ran directly beneath the windows of the parlour and the study. He noted as he did so that anyone passing into or out of the house by any of those windows would leave no footprints on such a surface.

From the path he found he could easily reach the junction of the two sashes. He also found that, by a little careful pressure with the blade of his penknife, he could push back the window catch. In other words, even if the windows were locked, it would be a comparatively easy matter to gain an entrance from the outside.

But to press back the catch was a very different matter to bringing it forward to a locked position when it was back. In the first place, it automatically slid in under a guard that held it until the guard was lifted and, secondly, far more pressure was needed to work it from that angle.

By persevering with his experiments, however, Malone made another interesting discovery. He found that a piece of cord passed round the knob of the catch and dropped down through the slit between the two sashes could be so manipulated that, standing outside, one could draw the sash forward to a locked position and then pull away the string entirely simply by digging on one end. But to do this it was necessary that the catch should be advanced a trifle under the edge of the guard.

Well, he asked himself, why not? Supposing someone with full knowledge of the internal arrangements of the house (as he had already conceded) should decide to murder Jacob Crabbe by the means that had been actually used.

Suppose further that this person had determined to make the murder as difficult as possible for the police to solve so that its very mystery would lend added weight to the suspicion which it was supposed to cast upon Gerald Crabbe.

With this knowledge in his possession, the murderer could easily carry out the deed, presuming that it was someone who could approach Jacob Crabbe without being suspected of any such terrible intention.

Once the murder had been done, what then? The murderer could lock the door and one of the windows. He could then fix the catch as he would have already discovered was necessary and then, after climbing out, could close the sash, pull the catch into place with the cord that was already passed round it and then withdrawing the cord, could leave the room in exactly the condition in which it was found when police broke in.

It seemed to Malone that he had found the answer to the question of how it had been done but he was at long way yet from discovering what brain had conceived that murderous intent and what hand had carried it out.

Nor were his interviews with the housekeeper and maid very enlightening. He found the housekeeper a personality quite as interesting as she had appeared when he had seen her first after the explosion. And, while she was perfectly civil, she could not or would not add anything to what she had already told the police, despite Malone's use of every tactful advance he knew.

But Malone was not anxious to press matters in that direction. It was the housekeeper who had given the police their lead to Gerald Crabbe. And she had been very closely linked with the dead man.

Not that this implied that she had had anything to do the murder. Why should she have gone to such lengths when she was to marry the man and thus, automatically, come into line of possession of his wealth?

On the other hand, it seemed that Crabbe had told her definitely that he had signed a will in her favour. If the copy in the safe was the only document existing of such a nature, then he had lied to her. But it might be only a draft, the completed will might turn up at any time.

Nevertheless, without that, things stood so that, as next-of-kin the three Crabbe brothers inherited, and if the housekeeper had been implicated in the murder then she must have been ignorant of the fact that Crabbe had lied to her.

In that case, believing the will to have been signed in her favour, why should she murder him? He was already more than seventy years old and she was a young woman still in the thirties. By the ordinary course of nature it stood to reason that he would not live very much longer. Then why should she take part in such a risky proceeding when she could gain all she wanted by waiting and living in comfort during period?

It was this phase of the matter that was the most puzzling to Lawrence Malone and he was driven to the conclusion that, if the woman had been implicated, then it must be because she was influenced by some other motive. What motive could that be? Might the answer be found to be the same as would name the murderer?

It was at this point that Lawrence Malone left the house and returned to London by train. But he remained only a short time at his house.

It was dark and a drizzle had already set in when he left again and, when he did, it was to appear in the disreputable guise which had so roused the suspicions of the taxi driver several bourn later.

During that time Lawrence Malone found that certain events he had anticipated followed the course he had expected. And the benefit of this was given in a telephone message to Inspector Latham, at his house in Brixton. It was one of the most electrifying messages the Scotland Yard man had ever received.

"Malone speaking," he heard over the wire. "I'm sorry to get you up at this hour but there is something I think you ought to know."

"What is it, Malone? It will have to be pretty good for me to forgive being dragged out at this infernal hour."

"Tell me something first. Did you leave everything in the safe at that house in Mitcham just as you found it?"

"Yes. But what on earth—"

"Well, let me tell you something," Malone's drawl interrupted him. "If you will open that safe now I am willing to wager you will find that someone has been through it."

"What the devil do you mean? There's a constable on duty there,"

"Oh, as for him, I fancy you will find him out of action. Better take my tip, Latham, and get in touch with the people at Mitcham."

And, in the midst of the inspector's spluttering protests, he re-hung the receiver.

CHAPTER TEN

Mr. Samuel Framer had overslept by nearly an hour.

It was a radical departure from that gentleman's habits, for he timed his daily round with meticulous exactitude.

But, then, it was not usual for him to be got out of bed at one o'clock in the morning in order to discuss business.

No one in the quiet road in Mitcham in which Mr. Framer lived knew that he was now engaged in any sort of business. It was generally understood that he was retired, that he was comfortably off and that his occasional departures for London were of no more moment than would comprise a day's outing.

And this suited Mr. Framer very well. Indeed, he took great care that no more than this was known about him for, although he had retired to some extent from active business, he still kept his fingers on the pulse of things and lent his son, who was his successor, the benefit of his many years' experience.

And experience as well as many other things were needed in that business for it was, in fact, one of the most prosperous channels for the disposal of stolen goods that could be found in the whole of London.

Scotland Yard knew "Frame the Fence" very well. For years they had tried to catch him napping, but Sam Frame had been too slick for them. It had been a bitter pill to the Yard to see him, after those years of illicit gain, quietly step out of what the general public regarded as a nice little legitimate business in Hackney and fade away. They believed he had gone to the Continent, and concentrated now on trying to catch young Sam where they had failed with the elder, they lost sight of their original quarry.

They did not know that, twice a week regularly, young Sam and old Sam met at a certain private club in Victoria, where the father listened to the son's problems, advised him out of his own vast experience and kept him posted, as it were, on the right percentages to offer his ever-shifting, stream of underworld clients. As Mr. Framer of Mitcham, an old gentleman with a wig where Sam Frame had been as bald as an egg, a beard where the other had been clean-shaven, and thick-lensed spectacles where Sam Frame had never worn any aid over his keen blue eyes, there was little to connect the two. At any rate, up to the time of the murder of Jacob Crabbe not a breath of suspicion drifted towards Samuel Framer and he would have gone on in the same safety were it not that, with a rich prize dangling beneath his very nose and an instrument through which he could gain possession of it, he could not suppress his old instincts. It was a mistake that was destined to prove fatal although Sam Framer did not know this until the bolt fell.

In common with the other residents in Sutton Road, Mr. Framer intended going to the inquest on Jacob Crabbe. That was to be held at eleven at the Coroner's Court, the body having been removed very early in the morning.

It was for this reason, perhaps, that any curious eyes did not discern anything strange in the police activity about the place from about three o'clock onwards.

There was a deal of comings and goings which seemed usual enough in such circumstances. Certainly, none of the neighbours dreamed for a moment that still a third extraordinary event had taken place in connection with that house of death. At least, none but Samuel Framer knew that the safe had been cleaned out and he was cognisant because, although his part had been passive, he had been keenly concerned.

It was this, indeed, that had caused him to oversleep so that, when eight o'clock came and he would ordinarily be up and dressed, he was still beneath the sheets.

But at nine o'clock he was sitting over his frugal breakfast and at a few minutes past nine someone rang the front door bell.

Mr. Framer employed only a daily woman to attend to his simple needs. At the moment she was rattling crockery in the kitchen, so, with a sigh, Mr. Framer rose to answer the door himself.

When he drew it open he remained quite motionless for the briefest space of time. So quickly did his hesitancy pass that none but the keenest observer would have noticed it. But Lawrence Malone had been watching for just some such sign and caught it before it passed.

Malone smiled affably.

"Good-morning, sir. You will remember, perhaps, that I was the person whose car was blown up in the street yesterday."

Samuel Framer nodded slightly.

"I recall you all right. What do you want?"

"You will understand, sir, that I must make a detailed statement to the insurance people. As you were an eye-witness it occurred to me that you might give me a brief statement of the facts and sign it."

"I've already told what I know to the police. I consider that you were criminally negligent in having a dangerous explosive in your car. You are guilty of the manslaughter of that poor coalman—if not of something more serious. I cannot be of service to you. Besides, I am engaged."

He made to close the door, but before he could do so Malone thrust his foot into the opening and then, placing his shoulder against the door, sent it inwards.

Samuel Framer spluttered indignant protests, but these died away into a squeal of rage when, without ceremony, Lawrence Malone shot out a hand, gripped his wig and jerked it clean from his pate, shot out the other hand and, in the same ruthless manner, whipped the beard from his face.

With these in his possession, Malone grinned widely.

"Well, well, well," he said softly, "if it isn't my old friend, Sam Framer. This is going to be a pleasure, Sam."

The fence's surface agitation was smothered at once. He knew now that Laurence Malone must have pierced his disguise before coming to the house in this fashion. It meant that he had overplayed his hand the previous day. He must have done something or said something that had set the detective thinking and, in fact, this is exactly what had happened.

He was quiet enough now. It wasn't only Malone he had to fear. It was the police and, as he realised that this man before him had it in his power to demolish all his carefully built ramparts of safety, he knew he must act swiftly if he were to save himself.

He managed to grin in return.

"So you've found me, Mr. Malone," he conceded. "Well, it doesn't matter, although I wasn't anxious to be recognised. You see, I have been living here very quietly for a long time and have wanted nothing of the world. However, come in and I will give you the statement you wish.

It evidently did not occur to him that Malone could possibly connect him with the robbery of the safe a few doors away.

Even if the detective had learned his secret it did not mean that he had discovered or suspected more than that. There was nothing, absolutely nothing, to link him with Jacob Crabbe's fate.

Malone laughed in return.

"You're just as smooth as ever, Sam. I must say it was a slick idea just to add an 'r' to the end of your name so as to change it and yet keep it near enough, at the same time. And you might have got away with it yesterday if you hadn't been quite so anxious to make things unpleasant for me. I wondered why you changed your tune only after seeing me at close quarters. It occurred to me that it might be because you had recognised Lawrence Malone. So I asked myself why a harmless old gentleman should have such an antipathy towards me. I began to think, Sam, and when I begin to think, sometimes I get results. But let us go along and get that statement."

The other led the way along the hall to a room that was the equivalent of the study in the house of the later Jacob Crabbe. Its condition, however, was in marked contrast, for it was as neat as possible.

The fence seated himself at a desk that faced the door rather than the windows and motioned Malone to another chair.

"Now, my young friend, what do you want me to say?" he asked, reaching for a sheet of paper.

"Why, Sam, I don't know that I want you to say anything. It's what I want you to do."

The other glanced at him sharply.

"Eh! What's that?"

"What I want you to do, Sam," repeated Malone patiently. "And I will be more explicit. What I want you to do is to hand over to me here and now the stuff that was taken from a certain safe last night about midnight and brought to you here. The exact time, if you'd like to know, was eleven minutes to one. Your visitor didn't remain long, Sam. But it was long enough to leave the stuff with you. Come on, my smooth friend, hand it over. It's a pity you couldn't leave well alone, Sam. I'm afraid it's going to smash up your pleasant little place of retirement."

This time, the fence's silence was distinctly more perceptible than it had been when he first saw Malone at the front door.

He sat as if frozen in his chair, one hand suspended over the paper he had been about to draw towards him.

But when his immobility did break, it went with a vengeance. With a speed that was amazing, he flung back in his chair and reached for the top right-hand drawer of the desk.

Even while he was hauling out the drawer he was rising and then, when he swung fully, his hand gripped an automatic pistol.

Crash!

The bullet thudded into the back of the chair in which Malone had been sitting, taking a line that would have drilled the detective clean through the heart had he still been there.

But Malone had moved as quickly as the fence. The instant the other dived for the drawer, Malone flung himself sideways, clawing for his own gun as he did so.

He was clear of the chair just in time to avoid the bullet that sped so truly and, when the fence's gun crashed a second time, Malone's exploded on the same instant.

A most extraordinary result followed. The bullet from the fence's gun ripped past so close to Malone's body that it cut away the cloth of the coat. Malone, who had fired to disable rather than kill, had aimed at the other's arm and now he saw the gun sent spinning from Framer's grasp with terrific force and speed as his own bullet struck it just in front of the trigger guard.

The terrific shock of the impact paralysed Framer's arm from wrist to shoulder. He reeled back until he struck the wall and there he stood cursing in appalling fashion while Lawrence Malone leaped towards him.

Malone wasted no time in a search for cord with which to secure his man. He found what he needed supporting a picture on the wall. He dragged this down from above Framer's head and, placing one foot against it, dragged the cord away. Then, swiftly and with hands that knew their job, he bound the fence, hand and foot. To finish the job, he made a gag, from a runner that lay on a table across the room and, when he had finished, he dumped his prisoner on to a couch.

But he did not set to work to make a search of the room, he knew that the sound of the shooting must have been heard if there was anyone in the house so, jerking open the door, he made for the kitchen quarters.

In the kitchen he found the woman who served Framer.

She was standing by the sink, shaking with terror and gazing fearfully towards the door by which Malone entered. The detective knew he was just in time. In another moment or so she would have bolted out the back door, screaming her fears to the world and that was just what he wanted to prevent for he had by no means finished what he had to do.

It was distasteful to him to prevent this by force, but he knew it was the only way, and her temporary discomfort was little compared to the issues at stake. So, allowing her to think him a desperate intruder, he seized her and made her secure. Then he locked her in the pantry and returned to the study.

No one knew better than Malone what chances he had taken in forcing the game as he had. If he was making the slightest error then he would be leaving himself wide open for caustic criticism by Scotland Yard. But he had been right in anticipating what would happen in the night and he was gambling that Sam Framer's visitor had come with just one purpose. When he knew the contents of that safe in the corner he would know whether he was right or wrong.

Half an hour later, when he stepped quietly out of the front door of Samuel Framer's house, he knew he was right.

CHAPTER, ELEVEN

Malone ran straight into Latham as he was passing the Crabbe house.

The inspector caught him by the arm.

"You're just the fellow I was looking for. I've been telephoning your house since seven o'clock."

"What's the trouble, Latham?"

"How did you know what we'd find here?"

"Oh, was I right?"

"You know darned well you were right. You knew it had happened when you rang me in the night. Come on, Malone, you've got to tell me how you knew."

"Why don't you demand the name of the person who did it?"

"Well, do you know?"

"I know who didn't do it."

"What do you mean?"

"The man you are holding for the murder of Jacob Crabbe. You've got the wrong bird, Latham."

"And that's where you are mistaken. We've got all the evidence we need against him. But there is something darned fishy about this, Malone. I consider it is your duty to tell me what you know."

"Not while you are holding my client on a charge of murder," said Malone, all the bantering tone replaced by coldness "As long as I am convinced of his innocence, I am entitled to proceed in my own way to make what discoveries I can, to keep those discoveries to myself and reveal them only when it seems best in the interests of my client. So I'll be getting along."

"Wait a minute, man."

Latham's voice was almost pleading. Gone was all his bluster. It wouldn't be the first time that Malone had sprung an unpleasant surprise on him and he didn't at all like the other's manner on this occasion.

"Well, what is it?"

"Don't you see that the man we've got must be guilty? The whole thing is so dead open-and-shut."

"It's too smooth, in my opinion. Just because Gerald Crabbe can't produce anyone to confirm his statement of how he passed an hour or so on a certain evening when his uncle was murdered, because

54

he has admitted that he was on very bad terms with his uncle and that he was in the vicinity of the house at the time the crime was committed, you at once pin the murder on him."

"Well, isn't that evidence?"

"Circumstantial—yes, but no more. Look here, Latham, if Gerald Crabbe had chosen to lie about his movements, if he had stated that he never travelled to Mitcham that night, but changed his mind and just wandered about the streets of London, you might have been suspicious of him, but you wouldn't have had a single thing on which to arrest him."

"You forget the threat he was heard to utter against his uncle when he was in the bar at Victoria station."

"Not at all. But what was that? How many times does a man mouth stupid threats and boasts when he is drinking, and Crabbe confesses that he had been taking a good deal of drink right along through the day. I don't place any weight on that unless you can show me where it links up with something more solid. I only have a few minutes to spare, Latham, for I want to get to a certain place before it is too late. But I'll ask you one or two more questions."

"Too late for what?" demanded the inspector suspiciously. "Possibly to catch the person who murdered Jacob Crabbe. Listen, Latham. Have you attached any importance to the condition in which the door and windows of the room were found when the murder was discovered?"

"That won't alter the case against Gerald Crabbe."

"Possibly not. But you may take it from me that, if you devote a little time to the windows, you should be able to draw an interesting deduction. And what about the explosion here yesterday afternoon? Do you still maintain that it was solely an attempt on the part of some of my enemies to relieve the world of my presence?"

"What else could it be?"

"Has it occurred to you that it might have been because someone wanted to get rid of me before I poked too far into the murder of Jacob Crabbe?"

"Do you mean that seriously?"

"I'm only making a suggestion. Here's another for you. What connection, if any, do you make between the murder of Jacob Crabbe and the robbery of the safe last night?"

"I'm quite willing to confess, Malone, that I don't understand that at all. We've got every available man working on it, and we'll turn up something all right. But you must know something, and I still think it your duty to tell me what it is."

"All right, Latham, I'll tell you. This is it. Gerald Crabbe did not murder his uncle. He is a fool and a waster, but he is not a murderer. The person who did the deed is still at large. It is the same person who robbed the safe. The reason the safe was robbed last night is because the murderer knew it was the last chance to get possession of the contents before the police took it away."

"But why?"

Malone prodded him with a finger-tip.

"Because, my dear fellow, because the murderer had expected to come into possession of the prize in another way, and that way failed unexpectedly. It wasn't a bungle on the part of the murderer, Latham. It was because Jacob Crabbe lied to a woman. Think that over, and you'll find the answer to every problem bearing on the case, and in each instance the same name will fit. Now I'm off. I'll be seeing you at the Inquest."

And leaving the flabbergasted inspector staring after him with open mouth, Malone strode off down the street.

Although Malone walked by the open streets his course took him, curiously enough, to the same house that had been his last point of interest in Mitcham the night before.

By daylight, it looked different from the unattractive small dwelling that had loomed out of the drizzle some hours earlier. Now it stood out as a neat, respectable habitation, and the clean windows and neat curtains within proclaimed the efficient and particular hand within.

It was, in effect, the very last place where one would expect to find the answer to sinister murder, but, nevertheless, as Lawrence Malone approached quite openly, he made sure that his gun was ready to his hand.

A woman who was whitening the steps of the house next door glanced at him with interest as he passed, for he was a tall and distinguished figure to be seen in that street.

Malone smiled at her pleasantly, but his eye was upon a long, low-slung, black saloon car that stood at the kerb a little way down the street. He noticed that its bonnet was pointing towards the main thoroughfare by which he had entered, and it occurred to his observant mind that it was sufficiently powered and well placed for one to make a quick getaway if one had reason to do so. It certainly did not seem to fit into its present surroundings any more than the man.

Malone pressed the bell with his left hand. His right was in the side pocket of his overcoat, his fingers grasping the butt of his automatic.

Scarcely had he withdrawn his finger from the bell than he heard a click that he thought was the turning of a lock, then the door swung open, but he saw no one standing within.

He was instantly on the qui vive. He thought someone was behind the door waiting for him to step inside. But, then, he knew that to be impossible, for the door swung so far open that it was against the wall.

Then, from somewhere in the interior, came a thin voice.

"Who are you, please? Come to the foot of the stairs and state your business. I am bed-ridden, and there is no one else in the house."

It was the pleasant woman on the steps next door who added her word.

"There's a sick woman there," she volunteered. "Her sister comes sometimes, but she must be out."

Malone thanked her, and stepped within, though he was still cautious. Despite his own suspicions, he did not want to rouse too much curiosity on the part of the woman on the steps.

But, the moment he did so, he knew that he had stepped into a prepared trap. The door swung closed behind him with a sharp bang, then, from the top of the narrow stairs, there was let loose upon Malone the most appalling stream of death he had ever encountered.

The racketing of the weapon was deafening. With the beginning of the stream, he knew he was up against a submachine-gun of some sort; and he knew that his automatic would be of not the slightest avail against that furious torrent of lead.

It was only his continued wariness that saved him. The instant the racketing began he threw himself to the right, crashing into a door that opened, he found, into a small parlour.

He dived into the room and attempted to use the door as a shield but that proved an untenable position for, as he sought cover, the person behind the gun came down several steps so that the stream could be directed full upon the door.

Malone flung himself to one side. The bullets were ripping through the opening and crashing into floor and walls. Many of them cut clean through the panels of the door while others became embedded in the outer frame.

No single man could stand up under that fusillade. It seemed to increase in fury rather than diminish and now Malone realised that his theory had been only too well founded. He had made a terrible mistake to come to this house alone. It was one which he might not now get a chance to retrieve.

His urgent gaze sought the window. He saw something flash past and guessed it was the woman who had been cleaning her steps. She was probably racing in terror to find a constable. But Malone knew that no single constable could save him from this predicament. It was one out of which he must find his own way, and quickly, unless he was to be riddled with bullets. And, all the time, that deadly stream of lead poured into the room.

Still he waited. He knew that, no matter what capacity the gun had, its drum must come to an end eventually while it was spitting, at such a rate.

Even now there was a chance that he could reach the window and break clear. But he remembered that powerful car that stood waiting in the street. His going would leave the way open for an escape that had been well planned against eventualities and his visit had come as the expected danger.

The knowledge that this had been prepared against, that it had been planned to shoot him down in cold blood should he become a definite menace, filled Malone with a cold anger. He might go to his death but he would only do so while trying to lay this arch criminal by the heels. For it had burst upon Malone now that he was dealing with no ordinary criminal, but that an idea which had been niggling at him ever since the night before was startlingly true.

Pressed against the wall behind the door, he waited for the moment he felt must come. It seemed to him that the stream of death had been rushing into the room long enough to empty half a dozen such weapons when, all at once, he heard the tell-tale cough. Then the racketing ceased.

The ensuing silence was tremendous after the appalling uproar. But it lasted only a moment or so. It was broken by Malone as he flung the door open and, gun in hand, dived for the foot of the stairs.

He saw something move in the gloom that enveloped the hall above. He dashed up the stairs, two at a time. Out of the gloom appeared the figure of a man. He was coming from a door that was directly in line with the head of the stairs.

He was carrying something that Malone guessed was either the weapon that had been spitting death or one similar. In any case he was working frantically to get it into action before Malone could do anything effective.

But Malone's gun was already up and now, as the other swung the sub-machine-gun round, he dragged on the trigger of his automatic. He knew a wasted bullet might prove fatal. And once that other gun opened up he would be riddled with lead. He shot, therefore, cooly and deliberately. He saw the figure beyond stagger back, saw it recover, heard a brief spluttering of the machine gun as he shot again, then the figure collapsed and Malone reached the head of the stairs.

CHAPTER TWELVE

The curiosity of the morbidly inclined was not to be satisfied at the inquest upon the remains of Jacob Crabbe.

The proceedings were of the briefest and most formal nature. Nor did even the Coroner know that the request of the police for an adjournment of eight days after no more than evidence of identification, was due to a note that reached Inspector Latham just before the proceedings were opened.

The note was from Lawrence Malone, was marked "Private and Urgent" and, despite his own conviction that the police already had the murderer of Jacob Crabbe in safe custody, was of a nature he could not ignore. It said:

"Dear Latham,—I am not attending the inquest, after all. I want you to have it adjourned and to see me as soon as possible. When I tell you that I am sitting guard over the murderer of Jacob Crabbe and an accomplice, perhaps you will do as I ask. If you do not do so, you will be making a grave error. I am sending this by a constable whose curiosity has been difficult to satisfy. It is only because I am sending him to you that I have been able to satisfy him. I suggest that you bring Inspector Garthwaite along with you, and keep the contents of this note secret until you have seen me. The constable will bring you to the place where I am waiting.

"Yours,

"L. M."

Therein lay the reason for the adjournment of the inquest but not the enlightenment of Inspector Latham. But, at the house where Lawrence Malone sat beside the bed of an invalid, with a dead body in the adjoining room, a revelation was awaiting him that was to force upon him the realisation of how close he had been to making a blunder that would have been an inky blot upon his whole career.

Latham knew, the moment he entered the house, that something of a very serious nature had occurred. The place reeked with the acrid fumes of cordite; even a casual eye could note the bullet marks that peppered the walls at that end of the hall.

The constable who had fetched him and Garthwaite had told an incoherent tale of terrible shooting, of how a woman had rushed into the main street adjoining to summon the police and how, on reaching the house, he had been admitted by Mr. Lawrence Malone who would give him no particulars of what had been happening but who showed the authority of a card from Scotland Yard and who ordered him to wait and take a note to the Coroner's Court.

Malone came down the stairs to meet them. After the first nod of greeting, he indicated the constable.

"Can you send this man up to keep guard in the room at the head of the stairs?" he asked Garthwaite. "There is a woman in bed, she seems to be an invalid, but I want her watched just the same."

Garthwaite gave the order curtly. He was not feeling too pleased with the dominant position Malone had assumed in the case and he was in almost complete ignorance of the activities he had been pursuing.

Malone led the way into the small parlour in which he had spent such a hectic few minutes not so long before. He waved an ironical hand at the riddled door and the pitted walls. Latham uttered a mild oath.

"What the devil has been happening here, Malone?"

"Sit down and I'll tell you."

The two inspectors obeyed. Both were eyeing Malone curiously. It seemed incredible that a man should have gone through that storm of lead unscathed.

"Now is the time for all good men to come to the aid of the party, and so on," said Malone in the same ironic vein. "In other words, it is time to ask formally for the immediate discharge of my client and to support my application by producing the person of the one who killed Jacob Crabbe. Well, gentlemen, that is exactly what I propose doing but, first, I must tell you that it will be a dead person I shall produce."

He turned directly to Latham.

"Tell me, Latham, do you remember a certain criminal of some fifteen years ago who was known as 'The Colonel'? He came into notoriety just at the end of the war and was sent to prison for a long term. I understand he died in prison six or seven years ago."

"Of course. His real name was Flinder. I was a plainclothes man at the time. I seem to recall that he did die some years ago."

"That is the man. You may recall, then, that even up to the time he was sentenced, there was a good deal of mystery about him. A lot of stuff never was cleared up,"

"I'm not very clear about that."

"It is true, you may take it from me. Well, the case interested me greatly and in the preparation of one of my books I had occasion to go into it rather thoroughly. I discovered quite a lot that never came out at the time of his trial. One of these facts was, that he had two daughters."

"I never knew that."

"Well, it is a fact. And, moreover, although the police were never able to discover his accomplices, because Flinder was most obstinate in refusing to give any information, I discovered the very interesting fact that his accomplices consisted of two women and that those women were his daughters."

"I never heard such a thing."

"I daresay not. But you are hearing it now and it is true I was vastly interested to learn this. I took the trouble to make further investigations and discovered even more interesting facts. It was the daughters who had been trained by their father in criminal science. He was one of the first criminals, you may remember, who used really scientific methods in his profession. He really had been a Colonel in the war and he was a man of considerable education and scientific training. Something soured him badly and he turned crook. He found very able assistants in his two daughters, and who must have been imbued with the same hatred of society. At any rate after he was sent to penal servitude the daughters carried on remaining in the background as organisers of a job while others carried out their instructions. But not always did they remain in the background. On one occasion they did a job together which entailed the use of a high explosive. This was a dangerous job of factory sabotage in the North which entailed the use of a large quantity of powerful explosive. There was a hitch somewhere and they were both injured, one of them so badly that she has been a bedridden invalid ever since. From that time they have worked along different and quieter lines. Both were married and the two husbands are now doing a long term in prison. The elder then specialised in taking employment as a housekeeper with elderly bachelors or widowers and using this as a means to get hold of their money by some means or other. She must have committed bigamy many times. And that is the woman who acted as housekeeper to the late Jacob Crabbe. It was she who murdered him."

"Good grief, Malone, how do you know this?"

"I'll explain presently. Let me give you the rest of the story. She wasn't long in Crabbe's employ before she knew of the nephews and the way in which the younger pestered the old man for loans. She was a good-looking woman and, I fancy, could bring a strong battery of charm to bear upon a man like Crabbe. She succeeded to a certain extent and got him turned against the nephews, so that he not only agreed to marry her but to make a will in her favour as well. It was there she slipped up, for he told her he had made, and signed such a will. She didn't know he had lied to her and that he was probably holding off until the marriage had actually been accomplished. And I fancy that, for some reason or other, he was beginning to cool off. At any rate, she grew so impatient that she could not wait longer. She thought about the strained relations existing between him and Gerald Crabbe and decided to go the whole hog, so to say. To encourage her in this decision she found herself in a position to carry out the deed in comparative safety. At any rate, she made her arrangements and killed Jacob Crabbe. Her alibi was one that was ironclad. If her sister swore that she had spent the whole evening there the police must accept the statement. And, through old association, she had recognised Jacob Crabbe's only neighbourly visitor as a 'fence' who had handled plenty of stuff for her in the past. Do you remember Sam Frame, Latham?"

"Of course. You aren't suggesting that he is in on this?"

"I am suggesting just that. Because the woman could give him away if she wished he was a ready accomplice to the extent of lending his evidence to hers that the door was locked when she called him. That was about as far as that went until she learned that the will had not been signed."

"But Frame—you say he was a neighbour?"

"Frame lived a few doors away under the name of Framer. He was disguised by a wig and a beard. He almost fooled me. If he hadn't been so antagonistic yesterday he would have got away with it, for my mind was on other things. At present he is lying bound and gagged in his study, and I shall be able to present details of a nice little case against him of receiving the stuff that was stolen from the Crabbe safe last night. But to proceed.

"The housekeeper decided that her last chance to get the stuff was last night. And here is where I was held up in the progress of my investigations. I believed all the time that there was a man concerned in the affair. It was only last night I discovered that the person whom I believed to be a man and followed for some time was a woman disguised. In other words, it was the housekeeper. She was a person of great strength of character, I assure you.

"At any rate, as the housekeeper, she was able to ensure that the constable on duty would not be a danger. She opened the safe easily enough. I was outside in the garden at the time. Then she took the stuff to Frame by the back way, after which she returned to this house to which she had received permission to come until after the inquest. This morning I called on Sam Frame and, after a rather spirited interview, managed to impress my views upon him. Following that, I came on here for, at last, I had the evidence that would clinch my case. You can see for yourself that my reception was a warm one. I walked straight into the full blast of a sub-machine gun and sheer luck enabled me to escape. As soon as I had an opportunity, I rushed the stairs down which the bullets were coming, still believing that there was a man to deal with. It was only after I had shot down someone dressed as a man that I found the truth. And, since then, I have persuaded the invalid's sister to fill in the gaps. So now, gentlemen, if you will come with me I shall show you the body of the murderer. After that I think you might gather in Sam Frame. I fancy he is feeling a bit cramped by now."

Malone led the two wondering officers up the stairs to the room where he had laid the body of Clara Deason. The bullet had gone clean through the heart and, of course, Malone had not known that the desperate criminal who had tried so frantically to kill him, and had not hesitated to drive a knife in an unsuspecting old man's back, was, in reality, a woman, for she still wore men's garments.

The other sister had been assured by Malone that only formal proceedings would be taken against her if she made free confession. And he was right.

But the same did not go for Sam Frame. Needless to say, Scotland Yard was highly delighted to catch this slippery customer at last, and, with the evidence that Lawrence Malone was able to hand over, the case against the old "fence" was ironclad. His sentence had been long delayed, but when he did receive it, the dose was a generous one.

As for the three Crabbe brothers, Gerald Crabbe was, of course, released immediately the truth was known and, as equal heirs of their uncle's property, they were able to remember their unpleasant experience with less bitterness.

And, while he professed to grumble at Malone for not sharing his discoveries sooner with the police, Inspector Latham was honest enough to confess that it was Malone who had saved him from making a blunder that would have been irreparable.

THE END.

[23400 WORDS]

ANOTHER MELLIFONT PRESS SERIES

160 pp.   Full Art Covers.   Best Authors.

Lightning Source UK Ltd.
Milton Keynes UK
UKHW041341211221
396027UK00001B/98